Endorsements

"In one of Jesus' many parable of wheat. Over the course of . centuries involving those who congregate under the umbrella of the church, there have been many ideals sown into our collective and individual identities that are simply tares. One of these tares is that of demographic segregation. As we await Jesus' predicted end to the parable, we who press forward as his students must dispelled the notions of racism and classism that so easily get planted among us.

"Jay Harvey's call is for this—to come to terms with the effects of these weeds choking us out and to sow that which the Good News of Jesus calls us to—being and becoming communities that receive each other so that we can love each other, as he himself demonstrated."

—Shawn O'Connor, M.Div., Anderson University,
Pastor & Correctional Institution Chaplain

"Too many of my dear evangelical friends and fellow ministers often unwittingly (sometimes not) find their opinions and priorities more motivated by political ideology rather than sound biblical theology. Such is often the case for issues of justice, including racial reconciliation.

My friend Jay Harvey, through his own journey and self-discovery, articulately and convincingly posits that evangelicals, especially Caucasian pastors, are under a mandate from God to cease from binary, knee jerk reactions in the call to racial reconciliation. Jay's book is a heartfelt plea for embracing the possibilities by simply being willing to change."

—Dan'l Markham, Pastor, Author,
Radio and T.V. Personality

A Brief Moment in The Son

REDISCOVERING THE GOSPEL OF LOVE AND RECONCILIATION

JAY T. HARVEY

Author of:
Wrecking Ball: The Divine Interruption

A Brief Moment in The Son

REDISCOVERING THE GOSPEL OF LOVE AND RECONCILIATION

JAY T. HARVEY

Unless otherwise stated, biblical quotations are from THE HOLY BIBLE, NEW INTERNATIONAL VERSION®, NIV® Copyright © 1973, 1978, 1984, 2011 by Biblica, Inc.® Used by permission. All rights reserved worldwide.

Note: Some names and identifying details have been changed to protect the privacy of individuals.

Editorial Services: Karen Roberts, RQuest, LLC

Design Services: Mary Jaracz

Cover image by: D-Keine, istockphoto.com

Printed in the United States of America

For permission to use material or arrange a speaking engagement, contact:

www.jayharveyministries.me

ISBN-13: 9781689190206

Dedication

For Louis and First Lady "Bea"
You have remained faithful,
and I am forever grateful.

"The Spirit of the Lord is on me, because
he has anointed me to proclaim good news
to the poor. He has sent me to proclaim
freedom for the prisoners and recovery of
sight for the blind, to set the oppressed free
to proclaim the year of the Lord's favor."
Luke 4:18–19

FOREWORD

As Christians, we must embark upon a path that will lead us into direct confrontation with the myth that elevates whiteness as superior. This social construct is destroying us all, regardless of ethnicity.

It's time for the body of Christ to deal with the uncomfortable racial hierarchy that has been the basis for the structure of our entire society and the role it's played in its construction.

As the founding pastor of United In Christ Church in Anderson, IN, for over twenty-two years I have been using my voice to call the body of Christ to unite and become the salt and light we are chosen to be. The reason why we haven't solved the racial divide in America after hundreds of years is because people apart from God are trying to invent unity, while the people who belong to God are not living out the unity we already possess in Christ. I am convinced there needs to be an awakening to what it means to be a disciple of Jesus Christ and the cost that ensues.

I believe Jay Harvey has been chosen by God to help lead the way by dealing with the issue of reconciliation. I've known about Jay Harvey for several years, and in most recent years I have come to know him as my brother in Christ. I've observed him in many situations and conversations about reconciliation and justice, and

I can attest that he is attuned to his own identity and privilege as a white man.

I have seen Jay's convictions cost him and his family a great deal, but he has never wavered from what he believes God has called him to. He realizes that when you begin to speak out against the establishment, the establishment fights back; nevertheless he has remained faithful to the call to be a voice for reconciliation. Despite his doubts and struggles at times, he knows that God called him to write this book.

A Brief Moment in the Son is a call to follow Jesus and become ministers of love and true reconciliation. This book will lead people on a transformational journey as they renew their minds to the truth.

Let's bask in the Son...together.

—*Louis C. Jackson, Jr.*

Contents

A Word about the Title

W. E. B. Du Bois was a prominent voice as an African American sociologist, writer, and activist during his lifetime (1868–1963). Du Bois had a unique way of bringing clarity to the moment in the way he wrote and spoke. Seeing the reality of what was happening in the post-slavery Jim Crow era, Du Bois uttered these words: "the slave went free; stood a brief moment in the sun; then moved back again towards slavery."

The title and contents of this book are meant to provide a moment of clarity for the body of Christ. The opportunity that exists for bringing the body of Christ into a new unity is right in front of our eyes. The time is now, but it will require some honest conversation.

The gospel is meant to set free and unite all who accept it, and yet too often the classism that still exists in the modern-era church provides only "a brief moment" of equality and dignity for people of color, the poor, and the marginalized. Or, put more bluntly, a new believer is welcomed into the family of God, but then their skin color, class, and societal status determine their place in the church. Most are relegated to their proper place according to classism, with no experience of ever being equal with others in the body of Christ who have a different status.

No matter who you are, where you come from, or what your lot in life is, the ground at the cross is level. Standing on level ground and being united in Christ with all other believers is meant to bring kinship, reconciliation, and equality. Jesus' death and resurrection brought down the wall of hostility that divided humankind. The cross makes all who are in Christ one family, and as ambassadors for the kingdom of God, we are called to the ministry of reconciliation.

Today's contemporary Christian lives and breathes in a culture that is still status driven. The poor, the marginalized, and those of different ethnicities are celebrated for their faith for what amounts to a "brief moment in the Son" but then relegated back to their place in society. This inequality must change. I pray this book will help bring us to a place where we can all stand in the "Son" together and stay there together.

Preface

In 1999 I stood in a baptismal in front of a packed church. Many who were there that day probably wondered silently what kind of deal I was trying to make with God. There was no deal. It was simple. I had finally waved the white flag and said, "Lord, please save me."

As I emerged from the waters with the help of my pastor, Jim Lyon, I had no idea what the future held. I stood motionless and dripping wet, hoping no one could tell the difference between water and the tears streaming down my face. My insecurities quickly faded, however, because I realized for the first time in my life, I had peace.

Twenty years later, the peace I found in Christ on that day remains secure. Everything else, however, has been tested, shaken, and refined.

Call to Ministry

God called me to full-time ministry in 2001 with a specificity that to this day I remember word for word. For the next few years, I was immersed in God's word, leading Bible studies and services at the local jail. I served as a liaison for college students at my local church and did development work for a parachurch ministry.

The areas of ministry I was involved in were helping me grow, and I sensed more was coming. Deep inside my heart, I knew God was leading me to a bigger platform for ministry. It was hard to verbalize, but I just knew it was coming.

Fast forward to 2011. I was called to serve as senior pastor for a large, suburban church. I served nearly six years and celebrated over 300 baptisms. Some were new believers, some were church members whose faith had come alive, and some were recommitments to Christ. It was an exciting time.

Great things were happening as people came alive in their faith, but at the same time there was an unsettledness in my spirit that was starting to grow. It was a nagging little uncertainty about the future of the church—not only the church I was pastoring, but the overall body of Christ in general. I could see the tension between authenticity and too much reliance on structure, or the "business model." I don't mind structure at all. But when it comes at the expense of relationship, truth, and the gospel, all bets are off.

The gospel has consequences, and so does following Jesus. The tension grew and ultimately led me to question some of my own motivations. Had I become too reliant on systems or too reliant on myself? What was I missing? I was getting more and more numb to the world outside but didn't know why.

In May 2016, I was scheduled for a summer sabbatical. I hoped the time away would provide me the time and space I needed to figure out why my spirit was troubled and, more importantly, what to do next.

In August 2016, I returned from my summer sabbatical. In February 2017, I resigned as Senior Pastor.

What happened?

I came back from the sabbatical rested, inspired, and ready. I also came back a different person. I had been reminded once again of God's love for the poor, the marginalized, and the overlooked. I had seen with my own eyes how far short the contemporary church, including my own, was failing in the area of unity. My fears about relying too much on the "business" of church as the way to control and manage the church were confirmed.

Not only was I reminded that church is not a business, but I was also convicted by the way in which the body of Christ is still segregated. I returned with a clear direction and mandate for the future that included less business and more reconciliation with our neighbors of color and with those who were poor. It had become very clear to me that diversity, unity, and equality in the body of Christ could never be experienced until racism and racial reconciliation inside the walls of the church became a priority.

I don't blame the elders or others for having difficulty with the change in my heart. The elders expected me to return with a renewed vision for their church. Instead, I returned with a burden. I came back having had my heart broken again for the poor and those in our society who have suffered under the banner of religion. I returned with questions about why the church is so segregated and why the body of Christ doesn't help each other in the way Jesus instructed.

I did not think I knew more or was more spiritual or more enlightened. I simply had a very difficult time communicating what was going on inside my own heart.

My prayer is by reading this book, you will be inspired and renewed as ambassadors for Jesus in proclaiming the gospel message of redemption, love, and equality. The potential that exists in the body of Christ when committed to reconciliation with the poor, people of color, and those who have no voice has no limits and will draw an entire new generation to the feet of Jesus.

How to Use This Book

The most effective way to read and use this book is to not draw conclusions but rather think and pray about the bigger message and the bigger picture.

The book itself is divided into two parts and offers questions for discussion at the end of each section.

Part One: An Opportunity for Healing sheds light on the issue of racism and the body of Christ's lack of credibility on the issue but in a way that allows the reader capacity to see from a new and energizing perspective. The book uses stories from Scripture and real life, and taps into the current frustrations that so many Christians may be feeling at present in the contemporary church.

Part Two: Reconciling God's Way focuses on how important unity is for the next generation of the body of Christ in the U.S. The later chapters provide ideas and alternatives on how to move forward as a set apart people who put "Kingdom" first and thereby changing the status quo.

Some suggestions on using the book:

- Read slowly and pray about what God would have you see and hear.
- Keep a journal near-by and begin making notes and journaling your thoughts and emotions.
- Make the effort to become an observer. Start paying attention to things people say and how churches interact with each other.
- When answering questions at the end of each section; be brutally honest and revisit the answers often.
- Be willing to give the book to a person of color or someone who you believe would be able to give you honest feedback about the contents.
- If using this book for small group discipleship, create very clear guidelines on what the goals are for the group and how to interact and discuss its contents.
- For more information on small group or other facilitation expertise, please email: jay77x7@gmail.com.

INTRODUCTION

Rediscovering the Gospel of Love and Reconciliation

To heal the wounds stemming from racism and classism in the body of Christ, the powerful and prideful must be willing to dip themselves in "dirty water."

Whether we like it or not, the church in the US is divided heavily along racial lines. This book is meant to address the need for the church to begin to model racial reconciliation and bring healing and unity to the body of Christ. The racial reconciliation of which I speak includes people of color, people who are poor (all colors), people with no status or voice, and people who are stigmatized in society.

Cleaning Our Own House

I believe the contemporary church in America has an incredible opportunity to be used by God to bring healing and racial reconciliation to our communities. The hinderance so far has been an unwillingness to listen to our brothers and sisters on the margins of society. Listening is difficult when there is an assumption you already have the answer.

My personal journey in rediscovering the gospel of love and reconciliation has been painful but purposeful. I have shed many assumptions that have guided me most of my life. I am still learning, but one thing I can say with assurance is that God's heart for reconciliation within the body of Christ is a serious matter. But it will not be easy. The assumptions and engrained biases that serve as invisible walls within the body of Christ need to come down and stay down long enough for "new wine" to be poured into "new wineskins" (Matthew 9:17).

God desires unity, reconciliation, and equality amongst His people. The means by which this change is achieved is not up to me. It's also not up to a denomination, a system, or those who currently believe their way is the best way.

When and if the contemporary church in America awakens to the need for healing in areas of race, classism, and prejudice, it must abandon all assumptions on how change will be achieved and who gets the credit. The method of healing can no longer be dictated by those who have allowed the wounds to fester.

In the body of Christ, the path to reconciliation will not be paved with money, power, or good intentions. Reconciliation with the marginalized, oppressed, and those who have no voice in our country will be led by God.

Revisiting Naaman

The story of Naaman found in 2 Kings chapter 5 is familiar to some but not all. Like many other stories captured in the

Old Testament, the story of Naaman provides a window into present day issues. I believe the story of Naaman helps unpack a conversation that needs to take place in the larger body of Christ in the US.

Naaman is the central character, a powerful and feared leader. He is prideful, intimidating, and esteemed by his peers. But Naaman also has an affliction that causes him to be self-conscience about his outward appearance.

The Scripture describes Naaman's affliction as leprosy, but it could have been any number of skin diseases. Suffice it so say, Naaman would like nothing more than to rid himself of this outward appearance issue.

Enter the slave girl.

"If only my master would see the prophet who is in Samaria! He would cure him of his leprosy." 2 Kings 5:3

Naaman gets hopeful and speaks about the possibility of going to see this prophet in Samaria. The King of Aram gives Naaman the green light and promises to send a letter to the King of Israel to vouch for Naaman and make sure things go smoothly.

Naaman gathers a large group of men, chariots, and a large amount of swag. They end up at the door of Elisha the prophet, and Naaman and his men, along with chariots and all the fanfare, are expecting Elisha to come out and wow them with his power to heal.

Instead, Elisha the prophet sends a messenger to tell Naaman to go and dip himself seven times in the Jordan. Naaman saw this as disrespectful.

But Naaman went away angry and said, "I thought that he would surely come out to me and stand and call on the name

of the LORD his God, wave his hand over the spot and cure me of my leprosy." 2 Kings 5:11

Naaman was a powerful person who expected a certain of respect when he showed up. Yes, he was desperate to be healed, but his expectation was to be healed with dignity. If you think that sounds absurd, don't be too quick to judge, because there's a little bit of Naaman in all of us.

Like Naaman, I can become frustrated when my perceived status is not recognized by others in a way that dignifies me. Yep, it just got real up in here.

Thankfully there is this thing called grace. Naaman's story takes a redemptive turn when he is convinced that if healing is truly the goal, then the means by which it comes is hardly the issue. Naaman decides to forgo his powerful reputation and go out of his way by humbly dipping himself in the Jordan River.

Coming up out of the dirty water for the seventh time, Naaman was healed.

So he went down and dipped himself in the Jordan seven times, as the man of God had told him, and his flesh was restored and became clean like that of a young boy. Then Naaman and all his attendants went back to the man of God. He stood before him and said, "Now I know that there is no God in all the world except in Israel." 2 Kings 5:14–15a

Biblical reconciliation is not fellowship or nice manners; it's kinship. It is the deep understanding that others have worth and value and within that worth and value they may also have something you need. Naaman discovered that true wholeness and healing came by allowing God to dictate the "who" and "how" and not to rely on power or status to achieve the goal.

Much like Naaman, who wanted healing and wanted it his way, the contemporary church in America often hints at the desire for racial reconciliation and healing. But because people within the church can't do it their way, and it may cause discomfort, they walk away angry like Naaman did. The result? Status quo.

Biblical Reconciliation

Long before Naaman, God had a plan to reconcile all people of all times to himself and each other. By establishing a covenant with Abraham and thereby promising to bless nations through him, God was initiating his plan of reconciliation.

God's heart to redeem and reconcile all that had been lost has always been inclusive but often is misunderstood. Yes, God set apart a nation called the Israelites, but this was not at the expense of other nations, but rather to ensure their inclusion. The Israelites were a fulfilled promise made to Abraham, and therefore, Jesus was a fulfilled promise to the Israelites.

As I sit and write this today, God offers me redemption and reconciliation through faith and trust in Christ, which was promised long ago to be the way that God would reconcile all nations to himself. I am not an Israelite. In the eyes of Old Testament prophets, I'm a foreigner. Yet I have been reconciled by the blood of Christ just like others who don't look like me, sound like me, or act like me. (Thank the Lord!)

All this is from God, who reconciled us to himself through Christ and gave us the ministry of reconciliation. 2 Corinthians 5:18

If in fact God has given every believer the ministry of reconciliation, then the body of Christ exists to be a proactive force for more than just evangelism. Believers' lives and their churches are commissioned to have a zeal for unity that comes from carrying each other's burdens and standing up for brothers and sisters in Christ who suffer from injustice, racism, and classism.

For the purposes of this book, it is important for you to understand my definition of biblical reconciliation. You may have a different understanding of what it means, but I hope it doesn't hinder you from receiving something new or at least adding to your understanding. When God speaks of reconciling us through Christ, we must remember its cost for him personally—death on the cross. Therefore, when I speak of biblical reconciliation, it is always about more than just "mending a relationship." It always comes at a cost.

Biblical reconciliation with a person or a group of people for the purposes of justice and unity requires accepting the costs of letting go of pride, control, and status. It is rooted in the deep understanding that others have worth and value, and within that worth and value they may also have something you or I can't find without them. Biblical reconciliation ends in kinship. The path to this kinship is time, grace, and a willingness to share the burdens of the marginalized in the body of Christ.

Part One

An Opportunity for Healing

Chapter 1

A Promise Kept

Sometimes keeping a promise isn't for the benefit of others; it's for you.

Doing stand-up comedy is not something you do as a hobby or a way to pass the time. You must be fearless, funny, and not intimidated by making yourself vulnerable. I compare it to walking barefoot over hot coals to get an adrenaline high. Yes, walking over hot coals can build your confidence and provide quite a rush. The difference between walking over hot coals and doing stand-up, however, is that during a comedy routine, you stand still, flat footed, on hot coals while trying to make strangers laugh. If they don't laugh, the coals get hotter.

In my late thirties, I decided to jump back into comedy and create a niche for myself in the art form of comedy with a message. It had been a minute, as they say nowadays. I would have to start writing again and practicing some stand-up to get back in the swing of things.

I remember briefly sharing my intentions in a casual conversation with my grandmother and her husband. I was just making small talk and didn't think much of it. About a week later,

I got a call from my grandmother wanting to know if I would be interested in doing a "funny routine" for the local Landlord's Association Annual Christmas Party. Before even thinking it through, I said, "Sure! That would be great! I'll be there; that's a promise."

Promises are funny things. They sound good when you are making them, and keeping them is always the right thing to do. Right?

I remember walking into the Country Club and seeing people sitting around tables, barely talking to each other as they ate their broiled chicken and cold green beans. This was not going to be easy. "But a promise is a promise," I kept saying under my breath.

Finally, after some landlord business that had to be done at the party, I was introduced. I remember taking the microphone and looking out at the crowd and thinking, "I am a complete idiot." I muddled my way through my material and found some bright spots here and there. I even managed to make the waitress laugh as she loudly cleared away plates and silverware during my act.

As promises go, that one was a killer. I persevered, however, and continued to expand my ministry with comedy, writing, and speaking. A promise kept, no matter how hard or painful to fulfill, can change the course of your life.

A Promise Kept

From July 2011 to May 2016, I served as the senior pastor of a church in a wonderful community outside of Indianapolis. It was a wonderful time of personal growth in addition to growth in the church.

In the spring 2016, I was gifted a sabbatical for the summer months. I was eager to rest, pray, and catch my breath. I truly wanted to use the time away to process what the church would need to be in the coming years to meet the changing culture with the good news of Christ.

What most people didn't know is that I had already begun to wrestle in my own heart with how we did certain things in the church. We were relying on the same old while continually comparing ourselves to other churches and ministries. I felt an increasing conviction that God was not happy with how we were measuring our success. I didn't say much about my feelings at the time because I was getting ready to go on sabbatical and just figured I would deal with them then.

The first few days of my sabbatical, I prayed and asked God what to read. I was eager to reconnect with the Bible in a way that sometimes is difficult for pastors. I know it sounds odd, but I was seeking a fresh connection with God's Word. I wanted to lose track of time and not worry about upcoming appointments or sermon prep. I had been studying so long and writing so many papers that I was ready to be wooed again.

As I prayed about what to read, Jeremiah kept coming to mind. Not my first choice, but after about the third prompting of the Holy Spirit to open the book of Jeremiah, I got out my Bible and began to read. A verse in chapter 2 leapt off the page and hit me square in the face.

"My people have committed two sins: They have forsaken me, the spring of living water, and have dug their own cisterns, broken cisterns that cannot hold water." Jeremiah 2:13

Reading those words in Scripture jolted me. It was like getting the feeling back in an area of your body that had been numb, which can be uncomfortable at first but on the other hand reminds us that we are alive.

The verse references two sins, and I think it's worth noting that the first sin leads to the second one. By turning away from the true source of living water, God's people are left to rely on their own strength or, as the Scripture puts it, man-made cisterns. Jeremiah points out that these man-made cisterns are broken and cannot even hold water.

With this verse, God had begun the process of revealing why I was wrestling with certain aspects of the overall church. People turning away from God, even when they don't realize they are doing it. Relying on a different source of strength to give them their identity.

Today's believers rely on denomination, tradition, status, politics, and race as their primary identity in Christ. Although it was painful to admit that I too had fallen into this trap, it was also comforting to know God's grace was allowing me to see the path forward. The path forward was not innovative marketing or some radical new idea, but rather the simple returning to Jesus in Luke 4, who proclaimed who he was and why he had come.

Two weeks into my sabbatical, I drove to North Carolina to attend The Summer Institute for Reconciliation hosted at Duke Divinity School. It was the tenth anniversary of the founding of the seminar, and I was eager to connect with others and discuss God's heart for biblical reconciliation. The first morning of the seminar, the opening speaker informed us that most of the week would focus on Lamentations and parts of Jeremiah. I fell out of my chair.

While I was there, I was privileged to sit under the teaching of those who had spent their lives dealing with issues related to racial reconciliation in the church from around the world. One of my instructors challenged me with a task that would prove to be the catalyst moment in my life of ministry.

"It surprises me that more of you who are white don't have mentors of color," she said. "I hope when you return home, you will reach out and find a mentor of color and just sit at their feet and listen."

I was thinking to myself, "What an odd thing to say. A mentor is a mentor no matter the color of their skin." As the week progressed, however, I sensed that God was using the experience at Duke to open me up to something new. My angst about the modern-era mind-set of the overall church, combined with the Jeremiah Scripture verse, had awakened me to something that would change the course of my life.

I realized my spiritual numbness was wearing off, and it had nothing to do with learning a new leadership technique or coming up with the perfect 5-year plan for the church. My eyes had been opened again to what God wanted me to see. It was scary but invigorating, and there was no turning back. God seemed to be calling me to be a voice of reconciliation and justice in a new way. I would have to lay down all my assumptions and be willing to listen and learn. And the only way I could see this happening was to accept my instructor's challenge to find a mentor of color. So, I promised myself when I got back home, I would do exactly that.

Reconciliation, specifically racial reconciliation as the way to bring new life to the church, was exciting to me because it would force the status quo to change. Pursuing racial reconciliation and social justice is certainly not a new concept, and over the years the church and other societal agencies have made strides in bringing people together. But we in the body of Christ are still a long way off from God's idea of modeling reconciliation to the world, especially when it pertains to race.

Another Promise Kept

Remember, a promise is a promise, and a kept promise can change the course of your life.

After the weeklong intensive on reconciliation was over, I got in my car and began the long drive back home. I prayed, cried, and knew that God had opened something new in me that could never be closed. I took some time to decompress once I got home and then began to pray about who God wanted me to meet with and pursue as a mentor.

The answer to my prayers in more ways than one was a man named Louis Jackson Jr. So, I emailed a request to meet with pastor Louis Jackson.

I knew of Pastor Jackson (Pastor J), but simply as a peer. Most pastors are not good at getting together with other pastors to get to know one another better. Our relationships with one another are distant and surface at best because the harsh reality is that there is only so much emotional capacity a pastor can possess. Befriending other pastors would call for an extra-large additional portion.

My meeting with Pastor J was going to be crucial for applying what I had learned at Duke. I told him I wanted to come to his office. He agreed. If God was truly calling me to be a voice for justice and reconciliation in my hometown, I would need to learn as much as possible about the racial divide in the body of Christ.

When I arrived, I politely knocked on his office door and in return I heard, "Come on in, Pastor. I'm here." When I opened the door, I was met with a "bear hug" that to this day causes me to wheeze when I take a deep breath!

The office had all the characteristics of a war room for someone who had spent years in the fight for souls. Hundreds of books and papers lined the bookshelves, and several inspirational pictures and framed Scriptures hung on the walls. The one book that stood out among the others was placed in the middle of his desk. The Bible. I learned quickly that the Word of God had been and would always be Pastor J's primary ally in the quest for unity and equality in the body of Christ.

After the bear hug (did I mention it still hurts?), he invited me to sit at a table in the middle of the room. The table was a rectangle with a chair at each end. For a split second I thought I heard the soundtrack of *The Godfather* playing in the background. If at any point Pastor J would have said, "I'm going to make you an offer you can't refuse," I would have replied, "Don't worry, I'm on your side, and besides, I don't own a horse."

After sitting down, Pastor J at one end and me at the other, he looked at me, lowered his head so he could look at my eyes from over the top of his bifocal glasses, and said, "I'm just going to get to the point. I have white pastors calling me all the time wanting to meet and talk about reconciliation, justice, and unity. Then they proceed to instruct me on how it needs to be done without even asking for my input. I've gotten to the point where

I normally don't meet with them face-to-face because it ends up being a waste of my time. So, I'm just going to cut to the chase and ask you straight up. Why are you here?"

I need to mention that when he asked me this question, it came with a perfectly directed index finger in my direction so there wouldn't be any confusion as to whom he was asking the question (even though we were the only two in the room). My entire body tensed up. My Adam's apple refused to gulp. I was in no way fearful, but rather it was the weight of the moment that struck me. I knew my next words would be the most important I had spoken in a long time.

By the grace of God, I responded to the question with brutal transparency.

"I don't know. I think I'm here to apologize for some past assumptions, and I'm here to listen."

Pastor J sat back in his chair with a look of relief and wonderment at the same time. He said, "So, you're the one."

I didn't understand what he meant by that statement, but I also didn't have time to think about it because he began asking me more questions.

"Do you understand what you are doing?"

"Do you understand what it will cost you if you truly believe you are called to this ministry of racial reconciliation and justice?"

"Are you prepared for what is about to come?"

As I sheepishly nodded yes to all the questions, I was also second-guessing myself. No sooner than I wondered if I had heard God correctly, I was reminded that something had been awakened in me that had changed me at my core.

I left the initial meeting that day wide awake.

After wrestling with what the future may hold and processing what I was learning in my ongoing meetings with Pastor J, I finally got a glimpse of where I was headed. It wasn't forward at all, but rather backward. Back to Jesus and back to the simplicity of the gospel message of love and inclusion.

To be clear, I had never left Jesus, but I can admit my Jesus was becoming much too predictable and self-serving. The Jesus I had been representing was the Jesus of my world, not the Jesus of *the* world.

There is no Jesus who is conservative. There does not exist a Jesus who leans towards the liberal side of the political spectrum. I have yet to come across the Jesus who makes it his mission to secure your right to bear arms. I'm also still looking for the Jesus who applauds one denomination while chastising another. Therefore, the first order of business in rediscovering the gospel of love and reconciliation is to revisit the Jesus who stood in the synagogue and said:

"The Spirit of the Lord is on me, because he has anointed me to proclaim good news to the poor. He has sent me to proclaim freedom for prisoners and recovery of sight for the blind, to set the oppressed free." Luke 4:18

When we revisit this Jesus, we return to what it means to be His body in our world. The body of Christ has been tasked by God to embody the gospel of Jesus Christ and therefore to provide refuge, hope, and healing for those in need. The gospel declares that believers living in other parts of town who are struggling with poverty, oppressive systems, and prejudice are our brothers and sisters. Jesus says they are family. Is that how you see them?

Chapter 2

A Moment of Clarity

The equality and freedom the American Constitution proclaims is not the same as the equality and freedom the cross of Christ purchased.

Racial reconciliation is not society's problem to fix nor the government's issue to solve. Racial reconciliation is the body of Christ's responsibility to model. *needs to be untaught*

If believers can "do all things through Christ," then modeling racial reconciliation inside the church is possible. As it stands now, the body of Christ remains segregated in houses of worship every Sunday across the US. Look at these statistics compiled by Pew Research in 2015.[1] *Jeremiah 5, 27+29, 6, 14+15*

Evangelical Church:
White- 86%   African American- 11%   Latino- 3%
Mainline Protestant:
White- 93%   African American- 4%   Latino- 3%
Mainline Black Church:
White- 2%   African American- 97%   Latino- 1%

The questions needing to be posed and answered in the modern-church era are why is this amount of segregation still happening, does it really matter, and what can be done?

I've heard answers to all three questions by a variety of people, and none of the responses are mindful of the bigger picture or approach the issue from a kingdom of God mind-set. Churches are quick to talk about the kingdom, but when it comes down to implementation, the definition of kingdom gets smaller.

A kingdom-minded discussion on the issues of racial reconciliation in the body of Christ must first include a better understanding of racism and how it affects our relationships. A kingdom-minded discussion must not settle for answers too quickly, as it takes time to understand and process what God desires.

It's easy to identify racism if it is viewed only as an issue of color. Racism in the US may have its roots in skin color, but today more than ever it is about economics, class, and power. It doesn't matter what color you are when others don't see you as a person who has worth or value.

Racial things R sensitive

A Painful Snapshot of How Far We Haven't Come

"Can't we just get along?"

These infamous words are from a man in Los Angeles in 1991 who was thrust into the spotlight by taking a beating from four white police officers. His name was Rodney Glen King III, an African American taxi driver in southern California. For many Americans, the name Rodney King will forever be a symbol of racial tensions in America and a marker to measure progress or the lack thereof in race relations.

The story of Rodney King, like so many other stories involving race, is merely a symptom of a much bigger issue. The issue is more complex than racism. The issue is what prolific author and pastor Howard Thurman refers to as the fate of "the disinherited."

Thurman says, "It cannot be denied that too often the weight of the Christian movement has been on the side of the strong and powerful and against the weak and oppressed—this despite the gospel."[2]

Lurking beneath the surface of every marginalized segment of society is the realization that in spite of the gospel, in spite of all social justice initiatives, and in spite of the narrative that all are equal and free, some are still disinherited. Therefore, when an episode of social injustice or racial bias is on the front page, whether accurately reported or not, it adds one more straw to the camel's back. Eventually an explosive or tragic event occurs, and all hell breaks loose. The event itself is the tipping point, and while the disinherited show their frustration, those in power do their best to convince those on the margins of society why they are wrong to be frustrated. A vicious cycle.

In a very real sense, what happened to Rodney King revealed the hearts of millions of Americans and revealed how little progress had been made in the racial reconciliation stemming from the civil rights movement, a movement many adopted as a gospel-centric, coming-of-age movement. Unfortunately, the body of Christ in large part has reverted to the comfort of class, status, and hierarchy. Today's segregated churches are proof that not much has changed.

A Perspective

Rodney King did not stop when police tried to pull him over. When he was finally stopped and emerged from his car, officers could see he was intoxicated. Initially King was not displaying the behavior police officers desire when securing a scene, which also included the presence of two other gentlemen who were intoxicated. As a result, four officers surrounded King and began to subdue him. Then they began using excessive force. The officers clubbed him repeatedly as someone from across the street on a second-floor terrace captured the entire event on video.

Rodney King leading the law enforcement officers on a high-speed chase and having to be pulled over was a mistake. Rodney King driving while intoxicated was a mistake. The bigger picture that would soon emerge, however, would once again reveal the hearts of many in how far our country had *not* come in racial reconciliation. The Rodney King video and ensuing violence was a moment of clarity that once again revealed a deep-seated frustration and distrust that the disinherited have for those in power and the justice system.

Unintended Consequences

The events captured on video between Rodney King and the police officers led to a trial for the four white officers. The consequences and casualties stemming from the not guilty verdicts for the four officers resulted in the deaths of more than fifty people. Hundreds of additional people were injured, and millions of dollars of damage to businesses happened from the ensuing riots, vandalism, and arson.

You might be thinking, "Nobody forced those people to riot." You would be right. But they did.

I'm sure some in the body of Christ decided in 1992 to do whatever was necessary to bring people together without blame or pointing fingers. But it was not enough.

The question that haunts me is why, after more than twenty-five years, not much has changed.

February 26, 2012: Trayvon Martin, an African American age fifteen, was shot dead by an overzealous "neighborhood watch" citizen named George Zimmerman.

Take a moment and put yourself in this situation. What happened? Who was at fault?

Zimmerman was told repeatedly by 911 operators to stop pursuit. He did not comply. Zimmerman continued to pursue Trayvon Martin. Did Trayvon become fearful? Is it possible Trayvon thought someone was following him and that's why he was trying to avoid a confrontation? I don't know the answers. You don't know the answers either.

You might think, by watching the news and the outcome of the trial that ended in Zimmerman being found not guilty, that justice was done. The lingering effect being overlooked is the bigger issue. The lurking, ever-present truth is that some are still disinherited. The African American community believes only this about the scenario: another young black male is shot dead, another not guilty verdict is handed down by the justice system, and a long list of questions as to why follow.

<u>August 9, 2014</u>: Michael Brown, an African American teenager, was shot six times and killed by a white police officer. Justified or not, provoked or not provoked, this shooting was yet another episode that allowed deep-seated feelings and beliefs to erupt. This time the riots started even before the decision came on whether to indict the officer who shot Michael Brown.

Nobody from a legal standpoint can dispute that Michael Brown agitated a situation that was already escalating. I don't exonerate Brown for committing a crime, nor do I assign evil intent by the officer who shot him. What about you?

It's time for the body of Christ to step in and seize the opportunity to engage in the right conversations about these matters. The unanswered questions regarding Michael Brown and Trayvon Martin are not about who was right and who was wrong. They are about how young black men and others who see themselves as marginalized and forgotten will find an alternative hope and future that dignifies their humanity.

The gospel of Jesus Christ provides everything needed to remedy these issues.

If the body of Christ in the US could begin having the big picture conversation about racism with a commitment to not rest until "reconciled and healed" is the new status quo, others who consider themselves disinherited would finally see the hope they've been waiting to experience.

It's Me; It's You; It's All of Us

A hard pill to swallow for most of us is sometimes there isn't a clear answer for problems that desperately need a clear answer.

It is especially hard for people who think logically and have a very structured worldview. Unfortunately, the quest for a logical answer to a spiritual problem will always be elusive; yet the modern-era church continues to rely on logic, structure, and worldview assumptions to address heart issues.

Heart issues have never been solved through laws or logic. Heart issues, especially in the body of Christ, can't be programmed into healing. There must be a moment of awareness, followed by repentance, before change will come.

It is no surprise that God emphasizes relationship as part of reconciliation. The Bible from start to finish is about relationship. First and foremost, you and I are reconciled to God through Christ and put back in a right relationship with God. When we become believers in Christ and participants in the kingdom, God sees us as reconcilers as well.

There is no avoiding the call to be a reconciler. If you think you are exempt, read the Sermon on the Mount again.

God's heart for reconciliation is in no way a segregated reconciliation or a partial reconciliation. When Jesus died on the cross to redeem that which was lost and reconcile us to the Father, there was no thought for race, class, or status. A poor Christian is your kin. A black Christian is your kin. A homeless Christian who is struggling to survive an addiction is your kin. A Christian who currently lives in a prison facility is your kin.

Well-intentioned believers from all walks of life know all the right things to say and the right time to interject them when the world begins to come unglued by a crisis. Almost as common as discussing the weather, words roll off our tongues in the wake of a racial injustice or tragedy like, "Things are getting worse, and it's just a shame," or "I wish I knew what to do, but I'll be praying because something needs to change."

Yes, something needs to change. Or may I suggest instead of something changing, perhaps someone needs to change. Who? It's me, it's you, and it's all of us.

Do you know whose fault it is that our country is such a mess when it comes to politics, race relations, the family structure, and prejudice? It's me, it's you, and it's all of us.

Do you know who's to blame for such a lopsided incarceration rate among young African American males? It's me, it's you, and it's all of us.

Do you know who is at fault for hate crimes and homophobia? Do you who is responsible for the narrative that says the mostly white evangelical church has the right answers to fix society's ills? It's me, it's you, and it's all of us.

If nothing changes, why would we expect the world to believe in what we say is possible? Unity and equality in the church require coming together, being together, and staying together.

The more the body of Christ seeks the unity found in Christ alone, the more credible it becomes. The church can no longer use the same old methods to measure, market, and grow their churches and continue to think unity is the responsibility of everyone else to figure out.

Jesus brought down all walls and division so we can have peace with God as individuals and also together as the unified body of Christ. Diversity, equality, and kinship with believers of every color, status, and zip code would give the world an alternative future to believe in and a hope that would not disappoint.

For he himself is our peace, who has made the two groups one and has destroyed the barrier, the dividing wall of hostility, by setting aside in his flesh the law with its commandments and regulations. Ephesians 2:14–15

Consequently, you are no longer foreigners and strangers, but fellow citizens with God's people and also members of his household. Ephesians 2:19

Jesus is the first peacemaker in the kingdom of God. By bringing down all barriers, Jesus not only opened the door to become family but also the expectation for believers to seek ways to act like family. Sadly, the modern-era church has been hindered in efforts to truly reconcile and unite by getting caught up in one of the enemy's most effective lies: "You can be a Christian and still control your world."

Chapter 3

Be Still and Know; Be Still and See

Sit still and watch God work.

What does be still before God have to do with racial reconciliation? More than you might think. One of the reasons I believe racial reconciliation or racism is so hard to discuss is it's uncomfortable. It's also uncomfortable to sit still before God and begin to see or hear some things in your heart that need attention. That's why so many of us run around acting like we're busy all the time.

A quick peek into the lives of thousands of believers today could easily make the case that somewhere along the line faith, hope, and love have been replaced with anxiousness, worry, and doubt. When these three characteristics are left unchecked in the life of a Christian, they result in rivalry, competition, and anxiety. In the roots of all of these is insecurity of identity in Christ.

Anxiousness about life and all its difficulties can lead to worrying. The constant worrying about life, loved ones, and the future ends up causing doubt. The doubt most Christians deal with is not doubting God; it's not knowing what the future holds for them. Doubt ends up leading to feeling out of control. Attempting to deal with feeling a lack of control ends up with either letting go and trusting God or seizing control.

It's one thing to take control of your finances, job, or career path but quite another to try doing the same in matters of faith. Because Christians can take control over consumeristic choices in their life and fix their problems, they can make the mistake of thinking the same method works in matters of faith. You can begin to see why and how the modern era of the church is filled with rivalry, competition, and anxiety.

The gathering of believers once or twice a week to worship God is meant to bring relief from the harshness of competition and rivalry in the world. Standing shoulder to shoulder and worshipping Christ is meant to bring proper perspective and balance again. But ask yourself these two questions. Are you increasingly becoming more at peace or more anxious? Has involvement with your church become yet another area requiring you to multitask or a true place of refuge?

Let the Psalm Work

Psalm 46:10 has served as a soothing response to the question of "what's next?" for die-hard believers caught up in the age of the consumer-driven church. After long seasons of worry, busyness, and multitasking in their church, "be still and know" becomes a justification for resting until figuring out what to do next.

A closer look at Psalm 46:10 brings a fresh and new perspective on what is supposed to happen when we are being still and knowing. The answer comes as the psalm continues. **"Be still and know that I am God; I will be exalted among the nations, I will be exalted in the earth."** **Psalm 46:10** Without an ounce of my help or ingenuity, God will be exalted among the nations and in the earth.

In other words, from the moment I wake up in the morning, God is bigger than my day, bigger than my doubts, and bigger than my plans. And God is in love with the whole world, not just me. Jesus died for the sins of the world, not just mine. I live in a world where God will be exalted whether I am actively serving, stuck in traffic, or chewing my fingernails out of unnecessary worry.

So why are today's believers anxious and often filled with paralyzing fear? Why all the fretting?

Is it possible the worry and anxiety born out of an unpredictable and chaotic world is *not* being relieved as we worship together but instead magnified?

Is it possible that the competitive, consumeristic lifestyle has found its way into the body of Christ in America, and therefore, gathering for worship is no longer a place of rest?

Is it possible that the one place that is meant to provide hope for the hopeless, refuge for the weary, and kinship for believers has become a place where classism and competition flourish at the expense of others?

I would answer yes to each possibility, but I also believe there's still hope. Yes, the world is unpredictable and often evil, but worrying about it does not help. Neither does doubting God's plan for the future and seizing control. When we gather together as believers, we are to praise the name of God for the future that is promised to us. We are to see him working, not stress to manage his work for him.

Finding refuge and relief would be easier to do if every aspect of the modern worship service was not so choreographed. I understand why churches try their best to stick to a schedule, and it's not entirely a bad thing. With multiple services, campuses, and limited parking, it becomes imperative to turn over the crowd with precision so as not to seem inept. But is this creating more peace or more anxiety?

And then there's the competition. The desire to keep up with other churches and other Christians drives church staffs, boards, and leaders to be constantly comparing, measuring, and evaluating everything that happens. It's not a bad thing to care about progress and plan ahead, but when these goals get in the way of genuinely being still and seeing our neighbors as kin, Jesus and the gospel are missed in the process.

The competition factor is subtle, but it does exist. It has become very easy to size up and compare churches based on who the pastor is, the number of people attending, the style of music and worship, and how relevant the youth program is for young couples with kids.

Speaking of kids, the anxieties and insecurities that hinder believers when they gather for worship are being passed down to children as well. Children who go to church with their parents are sent to classes to learn more about a loving and forgiving God found in Jesus Christ, but they also see their parents attempting to serve a Pharaoh who demands more bricks with less straw.

Being still before God as Psalm 46:10 indicates will help individuals and the body of Christ to experience peace and restoration. So how long does the body of Christ need to be still? Great question!

Anxiety Is Nothing New

The Old Testament story of what happened at Mt. Sinai is one example of failing to be still long enough. Moses, the leader of the newly free Hebrew slaves, went up the mountain to hear from God. Meanwhile, those at the foot of the mountain became very anxious waiting on Moses to come back down the mountain with God's Law, and so they took matters into their own hands.

When the people saw that Moses was so long in coming down from the mountain, they gathered around Aaron and said, "Come, make us gods who will go before us." Exodus 32:1a

These former slaves had been freed from the hand of Pharaoh and sent on their way with gold, silver, and other goods. As they were being chased down by their former ruler, they witnessed God use Moses to part the Red Sea so they could escape. Not only were they free, but they saw with their own eyes that God would protect them.

Hadn't God also promised to continue to provide for them? Yet even after everything they'd just experienced and witnessed as they left Egypt, they quickly began to doubt and become anxious when Moses was slow in returning from Mt. Sinai.

Shouldn't they have been praying for Moses? Maybe standing in a circle, taking turns praying out loud? Always having the option of squeezing the person's hand next to them if they didn't feel like praying, of course. Or maybe somebody could have started working on a "Welcome Back, Moses" sign. Instead, in their anxiety and impatience, the Hebrews demanded that Aaron (the acting priest in charge) create something for them to worship.

The parallel for today is obvious. Christians in the modern-era church have been conditioned to expect their leader or pastor to create an experience to satisfy them and keep their attention. The narrative of "what's coming next" and the environment of busyness is much easier (even though it is killing our credibility) than being still.

Oh, how often I have witnessed a group of believers thwarting God's good purposes out of impatience and the fear of being still. The consequences linger for years.

Sit Still; Watch Me Work

Being still is uncomfortable. It often leads to self-reflection, and self-reflection often leads to questions. Some of the questions that arise out of a time of being still before God are hard to answer, and that is precisely the point. But anxiety, worry, and doubts about the future will never be overcome with more busyness, more rivalry, or more programs.

It's time to stop and regroup as the body of Christ. It's time to hit pause, lift the shades, and look outside. You may not like what you see, but as the numbness wears off, stay still and let your emotions become authentic again. Cry out to God. Cry out and be real with the Lord, and experience how the anxiety and worry turn from "self" to authentic lament and mourning.

I remember my affliction and my wandering, the bitterness
and the gall.
I well remember them, and my soul is downcast within
me.
Yet this I call to mind and therefore I have hope:
Because of the LORD's great love we are not consumed, for
his compassions never fail.
They are new every morning; great is your faithfulness.
I say to myself, "The LORD is my portion; therefore I will
wait for him."
Lamentations 3:19–24

God longs for these authentic moments. Lamenting or
crying out to God provides the opportunity to mourn our own
struggles and receive healing. It also gives us time to mourn what
our communities look like, how our children are more depressed
and anxious than ever, and how the church in many instances
has regressed when it comes to addressing racism.[3]

Remaining still, lamenting the desperation of others in our
communities, might lead to an acknowledgment that pride,
arrogance, and self-righteousness have led the body of Christ
to a place where repentance is necessary.

Yes, lament and mourning are uncomfortable, but as God
has promised in Scripture to renew our strength through mercy,
love, and a renewed identity, the world will have to take notice.
Dare I suggest that God will fill our church buildings once
again?

The biblical account of Hagar, who was Sarai's maidservant, reveals the power and the purpose behind God's loving encounter with a young slave girl who was disinherited and on the run. Why did Hagar flee? Perhaps a more intriguing question is why she returned.

When Hagar became pregnant with Abram's child, her status changed. Sarai was facing the fact that her long-time maidservant and slave now had some clout. Hagar had an opportunity for a new identity within the family and no doubt was eager to take advantage of the situation. Hagar and Sarai's relationship suffered because of the tremendous stress of a change in family dynamics of status.

The Scripture informs us that Sarai forced Hagar to leave by mistreating her. Being forced out was a serious matter because Hagar was a maidservant and relied on Abram and Sarai for food, shelter, and community. Not only did Hagar suffer emotionally from being shut out, she also found herself without resources, pregnant, and no hope for a future. But there was still reason to hope.

The Angel of the LORD found Hagar near a spring in the desert; it was the spring that beside the road to Shur. And he said, "Hagar, slave of Sarai, where have you come from, and where are you going?" Genesis 16:7–8

"Where have you come from and where are you going?" God already knew where Hagar was coming from and where she was going; however, God knew the value in engaging her in conversation. Being seen and being heard provide instant dignity for someone who is in pain. When a person knows they have been seen and affirmed by God, a divine strength is unleashed, and suddenly the strength needed to continue is ready and available.

Many people living in our communities today have been mistreated by the body of Christ. They haven't fled so much in terms of geography, but they have fled the hope of ever believing that they could enjoy kinship with other believers.

In a fast-paced culture, the desire to help the marginalized is often translated into actions tried without regard or interest for a person's story or struggle. The results are either short-term or ineffective. To bring lasting help and hope, the body of Christ must first allow the pain and burdens of others, especially those of different race and status, to occupy space in their own hearts so that biblical reconciliation takes root.

When trying to engage or reconcile with others without first understanding where they have come from, there's a risk of missing what God desires. Contact without fellowship deepens the divide between class and status. To truly help, there must be a commitment to see through the lens of the kingdom of God. God desires reconciliation; therefore, the call to love our neighbors goes much deeper than simply tolerating or being cordial.

She gave this name to the LORD who spoke to her: "You are the God who sees me," for she said, "I have now seen the One who sees me." Genesis 16:13

Hagar not only reveals that she has been seen by God, but she also says she has seen "the One" who sees her. Hagar, fleeing from the only family she had, has a personal encounter with the one true God. She has experienced being seen and cared about by God and immediately has a renewed sense of identity and strength. Hagar returns with the confidence that her purpose and identity are found in God alone and, therefore, relieved from all anxiety and doubt about her future.

Where Have You Come From; Where Are You Going?

A pivotal part of my journey in rediscovering God's desire for reconciliation came when Pastor Louis Jackson invited me to speak at his church. After spending hours and hours listening and sharing our hearts with each other, Pastor J wanted me to preach for two Sundays to his congregation. I knew what was at stake. I needed to be bold but not loud. I needed to be honest but not slick. I needed to share my heart but not make promises. I needed to let Pastor J's congregation know that I wasn't there to speak to them but to see them.

For two Sundays in a row, I shared my journey and what God was doing in my heart. I was bold but vulnerable. I spoke about the desperation and urgency that is lacking in the body of Christ to become unified. I spoke about the unwillingness of most in the modern, white church to pay the cost of reconciliation and how obvious it was to me that we are more divided than ever before.

I spoke about my engrained assumptions and how God was beginning to expand my biblical worldview. I preached on the parable of the Good Samaritan and how I saw myself as the "teacher of the law" who wanted to quantify how far to go in helping others.

After the two weeks of pouring out what God had been doing in my life, people came to embrace me, shedding tears. I promise you it was not because I had delivered the perfect sermon. The mostly black congregation had heard something different, and it had a profound impact.

The comments of a woman who was in attendance summed it up when she grabbed my hands and said, "I have been seen today. I have never in all my life believed a man like you could see me, understand, and connect with me." The power of being seen and heard by another person is important, but the power that comes from knowing you are seen and heard by the one true God is life altering.

Perhaps the time has come for the modern-era church to stop relying on best practices and logic. Being still long enough may lead to seeing the God who sees us and is asking two important questions: "Where have you come from?" and "Where are you going?"

The task of reconciling is not on the Hagars of the world. It rests solely on the shoulders of those who have been comfortable with the status quo and the segregated church. Being seen and reclaiming our identity in Christ will give the body of Christ the necessary strength to go back and reconcile in all the areas needed, with all the people who are a part of the family of God.

Reflections and Discussion

Walter Brueggemann, a renowned scholar of the Old Testament, encourages believers to resist forcing Scriptures to lay flat. In other words, the power and depth of Scripture is often overlooked when the imagination and literary form of it is not considered. He does not mean we have a license to change meaning or invent new interpretations of Scripture. Instead, he means believers do not need to fear making room for God's Word to say everything it's capable of saying to every culture in every generation.

Brueggemann writes: "What we understand about the Old Testament must be somehow connected with the realities of the church today." He goes on to say, "The contemporary church is so largely enculturated to the American ethos of consumerism that it has little power to believe or to act."[4]

A primary reason for why many of today's churches are even more divided based on class, status, and race could be linked to Brueggemann's assertion of how Scripture interpretation in the United States is largely based on our culture's consumeristic principles.

Let's look at one example.

"For I know the plans I have for you", declares the LORD, "plans to prosper you and not to harm you, plans to give you hope and a future." Jeremiah 29:11

It's fair to say that Jeremiah 29:11 is read by today's Christians more times in a greeting card than in their own Bible. The words have become so familiar that they have served as Christianity's own version of *carpe diem*.

The cultural mind-set of the American Christian sometimes has difficulty allowing this Scripture to be anything other than a personal guarantee for happiness or the relief of struggle. In the modern- era church culture in suburban America, Jeremiah 29:11 is often used as the excuse or temporary justification as to why certain aspects of a person's life aren't flourishing the way they planned. When an unforeseen circumstance or a period of the discomfort of not knowing the future interrupts the individual's plans for living life a certain way, Jeremiah 29:11 is the reminder that good things are just around the corner. Therefore, they mistakenly reason, it couldn't have been God who interrupted their plans.

Reflect on Jeremiah 29:11 and how it applies to your life. The Scripture can and will speak to you and your situation. Now take a few steps back and expand your view. In what ways do you see or not see the Americanized church allowing this Scripture to say all it needs to say to everyone—no matter what their class, status, or situation?

Jeremiah 29:11 in context is being spoken to a group of people, not just one person. God's people are suffering and are wondering if they will ever experience the tangible presence and blessing of YAHWEH ever again. Can you think of a group of people in your community who are wondering the same thing?

While some are reading Jeremiah 29:11 through the lens of their personal life struggles (which is completely acceptable and should be practiced), others are reading it through the lens of the struggles of their people and the problems they still face. The Scripture itself speaks truth to both, but interpretations are very different.

Imagine if I am in a men's Bible study in a suburban community church and one of the men shares his disappointment for not receiving the promotion he deserved at work. Jeremiah 29:11 serves as a smooth elixir for justification of what God is doing in the man's life. "There's obviously something better coming for you" is the consensus of the men, and once again the greeting-card theology approach has done its job.

Now imagine if I volunteer at a local homeless shelter and have a conversation with a resident who has no family, no money, and is in poor health but claims to be a Christian. What can I say to him to encourage or help? Does Jeremiah 29:11 sound like an encouragement? Or does it fall a little flat?

There is no doubt that Jeremiah 29:11 is an encouragement. It is a promise from God to give his people a future and a hope. Depending upon your status, race, and class, however, the future and hope are experienced in very different ways.

Discussion Prompts

Use the questions below the statement that follows to begin a dialogue geared towards a bigger picture mentality in the body of Christ.

Consider this statement: "As God desires reconciliation in all forms, the modern church in America can be repurposed as an instrument to bring hope, healing, and equality to Christians and others who are poor, oppressed, and victims of injustice."

1. Do you think those who are marginalized are hopeful about the future based on the above statement? Why or Why not? If so, how?

2. Do you think those who are poor and powerless can come to believe they have a place at the table or a voice to be heard? Why or Why not? If so, how?

3. Does the modern-era, affluent church do more "sharing" or more "teaching" (i.e., sharing of resources and meeting needs or trying to teach others how to do things better)?

4. How has denominationalism and biblical teaching negatively affected relationships with other Christians of a different race, ethnicity, and economic status?

Part Two

Reconciling God's Way

Chapter 4

Leaving The Palace

Moses tried to be an advocate for justice while living in the palace and failed. After leaving the palace and embracing his identity, Moses became the deliverer of a nation.

There is a cost involved in standing up for what's right. The cost comes in the form of vulnerability, risk of rejection, and sometimes a loss of status. As the cost or risk increases, the number of those willing to continue to stand up decreases. The desire to help others who are being unjustly treated is there, but few want to risk losing their position, status, or comfort in the process. Therefore, standing up for the marginalized in the body of Christ has unspoken boundary lines.

Moses and the Palace

The church building is not the problem. The traditions and encouragement that come from gathering together and being reminded of God's love are certainly not the problem. I believe the reason there is still division along the lines of status, race, and economics is because those in the majority are still trying to seek justice for others without being willing to risk their own status in the process.

In Exodus 2 we are introduced to the story of Moses. Before rescuing and delivering the Hebrew people, Moses himself was rescued by Egyptian royalty. The edict to kill all male Hebrew children had been given, but Moses' mother hid him and eventually released him into the Nile, hoping someone would rescue him. Pharaoh's daughter was the one who drew Moses out of the Nile and took him as her son. Moses was raised in a royal place, by a royal family, and was being groomed to rule Egypt.

But Moses was Hebrew.

No matter how big or how modern our churches become, it doesn't change our identity as sinners who have been redeemed. No matter how many systems the institutional church puts into place to become successful, it doesn't translate as credibility to those who are suffering outside the boundary lines of the comfort and privilege of the palace.

Moses was a Hebrew by birth, which means his people, the slaves, were treated harshly and often in the most severe of conditions. There came a point in the life of Moses when his two worlds collided.

One day, after Moses had grown up, he went out to where his own people were and watched them at their hard labor. He saw an Egyptian beating a Hebrew, one of his own people. Looking this way and that and seeing no one, he killed the Egyptian and hid him in the sand. Exodus 2:11–12

It would seem Moses was trying to do the right thing but was conflicted. He was a Hebrew by birth but had been raised by a royal family that considered themselves the ruling class, even to the point of being gods.

The story of Moses stepping in to help his fellow Hebrew illustrates what can happen when someone stands up for justice in private or without risking status. Moses didn't like what he saw but tried fixing the injustice without risking his position. The Scriptures reveal a heart that wanted justice but not at the expense of losing the position of privilege.

Much of what hinders reconciliation between Christians of different race, status, and culture is the unwillingness for those in power to risk their own comfort, privilege, and lifestyle for the sake of the kingdom.

Moses succeeded as a temporary advocate for justice, but because he tried to hide it and return to the palace without losing his status, the Hebrews remained hopeless. The next day when Moses came upon two Hebrews fighting and tried to intervene, his efforts backfired. Why? Because Moses had no credibility. They knew that after the argument was settled, Moses could go back to the comfort of the palace. Moses, like many of us in the contemporary, affluent church, try to help bring justice and dignity to others without risking our status or comfort.

Moses couldn't become the deliverer of God's people until he was forced to leave the comfort and prestige of the palace. Thrust into the wilderness, Moses embraced his identity and became God's instrument for freeing the Hebrews.

Let's get one thing clear. I'm not comparing myself or you to Moses. I personally could never survive in the real wilderness for very long, and the first time God turned my staff into a poisonous snake, I'd rethink my calling.

The Cost of a New Call

I returned from my sabbatical excited because God had done a beautiful work in my heart and given me the vision for the next season of the church. He had given me a burden for the poor and a burden for being a church that would become a model to others for embracing racial reconciliation within the walls of the church. I had assumed this vision would take place from the comfort of the church I was pastoring. I was eager to grow the congregation with the new vision. I was sure that our church would become a "go to" for racial reconciliation, the marginalized, and doing things in a new way that would actively seek diversity and unity.

I began to teach and preach to the congregation about the importance of reconciliation. Laying groundwork for the next few years would mean redefining the way we did church, and it would come at the cost of comfort in the process. In fact, I was so busy talking about it, I hadn't considered the cost I would have to pay. I was assuming a cost for the congregation without considering what it meant for me.

My insecurities surfaced after learning of conversations between staff and the elder board that questioned my integrity and my calling. I understood that my passion about the new direction may have seemed arrogant to some, but the burden God had put in my heart was emotional and urgent. The mistake I made was assuming others would understand and give me credit for the success of the last five years to move forward.

I learned much too late that others had been talking for quite some time and were never on board. I don't blame anyone for what happened. I had put the elders and staff in a difficult situation. My insecurities became a wedge, and the trust once shared between myself, staff, and elders was all but gone.

The cost became real for me one evening as I was seated next to my wife, having dinner with a consultant the church hired to assess the problem and determine a path forward. The consultant was scheduled to talk to the elders and staff the next morning but wanted to have dinner with my wife and me the night before. The elders, staff, and I had all completed a paragraph summary of what each thought the issue was and how to fix it, and the consultant had read everyone's prior to dinner that night.

Before the complimentary bread hit the table, the consultant said, "Jay, I think they all just want you to move on. They are ready for you to go." My wife's hand gently landed on my leg for reassurance. I realized she had heard the same thing. I honestly don't remember the rest of the meal or much of the next day, but I do remember the pain. To this day I struggle with that pain, and I don't wish it on anyone.

I did my best over the next few days to smile and go through the motions with the people who said they cared for me but were relieved I was resigning. The whole congregation was not yet fully aware of what was happening, and even though one of my mentors told me to stay and fight, I knew it could destroy the people in the congregation that I loved.

Let me be clear. My actions and inactions had played a big part in getting to this point. I had assumed much and communicated little. I had reacted in frustration and anger where love and understanding were needed. The vision God gave me for racial reconciliation was real, but it gave me no right to treat some of the elders and staff the way I did. For that, I am deeply sorry. I believe I was right in my concerns about being manipulated, deceived, and undermined, but the way I reacted revealed I still needed to grow as a leader.

In the span of a few months, I went from being excited, passionate, and hopeful to angry, depressed, and confused. The vision and burden were correct, but the location of where God would implement the plan was different than I had thought. Because of the pain and struggle, it became clear that it was time to leave the comfort of the church I had so grown to love.

Looking back, I'm thankful for the wisdom of God. I needed to become a credible witness for the cause of racial reconciliation in the body of Christ. The only way to get credibility sometimes is by leaving what you know and going to a place God promises to show you.

Reconciliation God's Way

Racial reconciliation that addresses color, status, and culture must be rooted in biblical reconciliation. Biblical reconciliation is an action requiring surrender, confession, and even repentance. Repentance for arrogance and for the way people of color, the disinherited, and the oppressed have been treated is where most Christians push back.

The story found in Luke 19 about a man named Zacchaeus is a beautiful picture of repentance, redemption, and reconciliation with others. If you are a believer who has grown up in the church,

I'll wait a moment as you finish the song playing in your head about Zacchaeus ("a wee little man was he") Is it appropriate to put "LOL" in a book?

Zacchaeus and his journey to repentance encompasses all the elements of reconciling God's way.

1. Recognition that something is broken.
2. Finding the remedy for what is broken.
3. Surrendering power for the common good.

Recognition

Zacchaeus was the chief tax collector, and Scripture says he had wealth. A wealthy tax collector who was a Jew meant that Zacchaeus had aligned with the powerful and extorted money from his own people. Zacchaeus used the system in place to make himself wealthy and gain status. There is no doubt that Zacchaeus was despised by his own people. Jewish tax collectors were considered traitors because they not only worked for the Romans, they used their position for selfish financial gain. Zacchaeus was wealthy, but most likely he was also bitter, lonely, and full of regrets.

Recognizing the moment when Jesus was near and wondering if what everyone was saying about this man was true, Zacchaeus took a chance to go and see. Perhaps Zacchaeus was at a breaking point and longed to be reconciled to his people and didn't know how to begin. Scripture does not speak about the motivation in Zacchaeus' heart, but what matters is the moment did not pass him by. The chief tax collector decided to risk his status and pursue something different.

Recognition of the moment is crucial. Don't let this moment in the body of Christ pass you by. The change you may be looking for begins with a deeper understanding of reconciliation with those in the body of Christ of other cultures, ethnicities, status, and color.

Finding the Remedy

Zacchaeus put himself in a position to see Jesus but couldn't. Scripture tells us that Zacchaeus was not a tall man. A large crowd was forming, and my guess is that the other Jews weren't very accommodating in helping Zacchaeus find a spot near the front. So the chief tax collector climbed a Sycamore tree (a bit undignified, but that's an entirely different book I need to write). Why a Sycamore? Low branches. Remember, Zacchaeus was vertically challenged.

Having climbed up in the Sycamore tree, Zacchaeus was now in position to see Jesus. Suddenly, however, Jesus was in position to see him.

When Jesus reached the spot, he looked up and said to him, "Zacchaeus, come down immediately. I must stay at your house today." So he came down ant once and welcomed him gladly. All the people saw this and began to mutter, "He has gone to be the guest of a sinner." Luke 19:5–7

There are some in life who are bold and cry out to Jesus in fear that they won't be seen. Prior to Jesus' encounter with Zacchaeus, the Scripture says there was a blind beggar just outside of Jericho as Jesus was nearing who cried out to Jesus to have mercy on him. The blind man was bold and would not be silenced. Jesus ordered the man to be brought to him, and he healed him (Mark 10:46–52).

Zacchaeus also had obstacles in getting to Jesus, but they were entirely different. Zacchaeus was an outcast for totally different reasons. He had become a traitor and lined his pockets with wealth by overtaxing his own people. Zacchaeus had much to lose, but he also longed to be made right with God and his people.

In some ways, the comparison between the blind man and Zacchaeus is a picture of the poor versus the powerful today.

Surrendering Power for the Common Good

Jesus is always ready to give the invitation to each of us to "come" just as we are and enjoy his company, but the invitation to Zacchaeus seems to have had more weight and urgency. Jesus said, "Zacchaeus, come down immediately. I must stay at your house today" (Luke 19:5).

I believe God is calling the modern-era church to "come down" from the position of observer and get back to an environment of intimacy and relationship with others. The remedy for what divides the body of Christ is found in Christ alone. Surrendering control and assumptions about how to reconcile is the hardest part. Much like Zacchaeus who was put on the spot by Jesus, the modern church must decide whether unity, diversity, and credibility are important enough to heed Christ's call.

The poor and oppressed in our communities who are Christ followers are waiting on those in a position to see and hear Jesus, to come and be reconciled through restorative justice and loving their brothers and sisters as equals.

Chapter 5

Retracing Our Steps Back to Jesus

To be transformed into the likeness of Christ, consumer-minded Christians must first stop trying to conform Jesus into theirs.

Societies change, politics and policies change, economics change, and we all know that feelings change. One thing that never changes is the good news that Jesus proclaimed. How the good news is presented and received, however, means different things to different people.

Getting back to the simplicity of the gospel will start the healing needed in regard to racism, classism, and other divisions within the body of Christ. The simplicity of the gospel restores the vision needed to see our neighbors again. The simplicity of the gospel illustrates and informs the body of Christ of the importance of reconciliation.

The Simplicity of the Gospel Can Be Complex

The proclamation Jesus made in Luke chapter 4 removed all barriers having to do with status, ethnicity, and economic standing. When Jesus spoke of this good news, everyone was impressed and hopeful.

"The Spirit of the Lord is on me, because he has anointed me to proclaim good news to the poor. He has sent me to proclaim freedom for the prisoners and recovery of sight for the blind, to set the oppressed free, to proclaim the year of the Lord's favor." Luke 4:18–19

All spoke well of him and were amazed at the gracious words that came from his lips. Luke 4:22

As usual, however, Jesus continued and made clear what the implications of this good news really meant. Next thing you know, the people were trying to throw him off a cliff.

How did it turn so quickly from all speaking well of him and were amazed at his gracious words to "let's throw him off a cliff"?

First, Jesus had more to say than just good news for the poor. He also proclaimed that he had been sent to set the captives free, recover sight for the blind, and proclaim freedom for the prisoners. Those who were in the synagogue had been interpreting Jesus' words to be exclusively for the Jews, but when they learned that the good news also included "others," they became enraged.

This mind-set is still present in today's culture but gets played out in different ways. The contemporary church in the West has focused on the death and resurrection of Jesus as the primary aspect of the gospel. The meaning of the good news is based heavily on the act of salvation, which is only part of the what makes the good news good. To go further, the entire point of Christianity for most in the white protestant church is salvation in order to go to heaven.

When focused solely on the eternal life and what Jesus did for us on the cross, the receiving of the gospel produces a life for some of waiting comfortably until that day comes. What about those who also are redeemed but aren't comfortable? The good news means something totally different to those on the margins of society.

Have you ever considered why inner-city churches are filled with emotional, hope-seeking believers while those who worship in prominent zip codes seek a Jesus to help improve their lives?

An inner-city church that is predominantly black or Hispanic will worship in and through past experiences and bare their souls in an effort to show devotion and love for Jesus. A predominantly white, mainline Protestant or evangelical church will worship with great passion, but usually it is somewhat measured, subdued, or scripted. The differences in style of worship are not as much culturally based as they are experienced based.

I'm not criticizing but trying to point out something that is not obvious unless you are among the disinherited, which is that the passion in which much of white America worships is limited by their lack of desperation for Jesus.

The difference in mind-set is addressed in the book, *A Many Colored Kingdom: Multicultural Dynamics for Spiritual Formation* authored by Elizabeth Conde-Frazier, S. Steve Kang, and Gary A. Parrett. In it, Deloris Williams is quoted by the authors because of the way she speaks about how Jesus' good news is translated and lived out in the lives of African American women in particular.

African American women have never thought of themselves as individuals whose goal is to attain their own freedom. Instead, they see themselves, in their efforts for survival and betterment, as moral agents who exist for the common good of the community.[5]

The authors also address many other cultures and ethnicities, including how the Hispanic community has their own lens for faith.

Mexican Americans have internalized shame and guilt as a doubly marginalized people. Moreover, struggling with their inferiority complex, they have come to believe that to be free is to become like Anglo-Americans in every way.[6]

The authors' point is this. As communities and cultures become more diverse in America, the opportunity for the mainline Protestant church to learn and grow in their mind-set can't be overlooked or minimized.

The good news proclaimed by Jesus is the same for all, but when the message gets politicized, Americanized, and institutionalized, the divisions between race, culture, and status remain entrenched. Once these classifications are accepted, they become nearly impossible to change.

Looking Over Jesus' Shoulder

The call to go back to the simplicity of the gospel message is so the body of Christ can rid itself of elitism and ask for a fresh lens in which to see Jesus and our neighbors. The parable of the

Samaritan found in Luke 10:25–37 gives us insight into how to move from our emphasis on salvation and go deeper into God's desire for us to bear each other's burdens.

Whenever I read this parable, I have a habit of picturing myself standing behind Jesus and peering over his shoulder. It's probably a subconscious thing that reveals my desire to be viewed as someone who is on the correct side of Jesus' teaching. It is difficult for today's believers to put ourselves in any other position because we read the Scriptures through a post-resurrection lens. But what if you were there when Jesus was approached by an expert or lawyer? What if you didn't know how the rest of Jesus' life was going to turn out? What if you had no idea that Jesus was going to be crucified and then resurrected?

Reading the parable of the Samaritan as if you were there is a great exercise. It can be even more beneficial if you are courageous enough to read it as if you are the "expert" in the law.

It's not much of a stretch to say the white Protestant and evangelical church in many ways has taken on the persona of the expert. When it comes to doctrine, methodology, and the emphasis on salvation, they appear to have all the answers. There's nothing wrong with preaching Christ crucified and focusing on salvation, but if we don't preach the whole story, we end up like the expert who asked, "Who's my neighbor?" (verse 29).

The expert's question reveals the heart of man, not God. Inquiring as to who exactly is our neighbor and who is not is motivated by the wish of not doing anything more than is necessary. The expert in the law, who had become so focused on having all the right answers, had lost sight of God's mission to redeem and reconcile all nations and all men.

I remember when my dad started giving me chores to do around the house and then eventually turned me loose to mow the yard and rake leaves. I remember wanting to please him, but when it got hard, I found myself asking for further clarification on the job description.

"Did you want me to rake both the front and backyard?"
"Did you want me to mow and trim or just mow?"
"Did you want me to mow once a week or once per summer?"

When it was 90 degrees outside, I needed to know exactly what the minimum was that I could get away with and still get my allowance. When the leaves fell (we had millions of leaves), I wanted to know how many "stray" leaves left in the yard was acceptable.

Everyone wants heaven, but when it gets hard to love someone or forgive someone or get uncomfortable to get the job done, it's easy to seek clarification about how to keep heaven without overextending grace and mercy, loving all and not just those like us. The business and "busyness" of the modern church has blinded its leaders and believers, who constantly seek to clarify how to be generous but not too generous and justify why someone deserves help or not.

Taking a Different Point of View

For me, reading the parable of the Samaritan from the point of view of the expert is always unsettling because for as long as I can remember, the expert was the bad guy in the story. What about you? But there is nothing to indicate the questioner was evil or was trying to unmask Jesus as a fraud. The Scripture simply says,

On one occasion an expert in the law stood up to test Jesus. Luke 10:25a

Drop all negative assumptions about the expert and put yourself in his shoes, or if you want to get technical, his sandals. Attempting to discern exactly how to have eternal life is something churches have been doing for decades in America, and most have learned how to respond the same way the expert did to Jesus: love God and love your neighbor.

Just like the expert, the answer has been engrained in our minds. But knowing the answer wasn't enough for the expert, and it still insufficient for modern believers.

When the question shifts to "And who is my neighbor?" (verse 29), the expert and many of us are trying to make sure we have a crystal-clear picture of exactly who it is we are supposed to love. Seems like a logical question because who wants to waste time and energy on loving someone that's not required?

Who is my neighbor for the church today is a question of efficiency. The church thrives on efficiency and has no time for errors or wasted energy. Who is my neighbor can become the first question in a long line of questions that self-justify and reveal the "expert mind-set." Another way to say it is that many of us are "testing Jesus" and don't even know it.

Seeking a definitive answer to the question of who is our neighbor can lead to these and other qualifying questions:

"How much am I supposed to give?"
"How often do I need to go to church?"
"Do I have to forgive others?"

Freedom is a complex issue. Freedom from sin and death is a biblical promise for those who are "in Christ." Freedom from bondage, being poor, and spiritual blindness is a promise made by Jesus himself. Therefore, if you are "in Christ," or in relationship with the one who made the promises, it would be a safe assumption that you have been set free from all these things and probably more. But does this freedom exist for all believers in your community?

Does the freedom that Jesus promises spread throughout all parts of your community, making everyone equally free? Or does the freedom from sin and death satisfy us enough so that we overlook the other benefits because they are not that important to us.

If a middle-class suburban believer knows they are free from sin and death because of Christ, they may not be as worried about the freedom from oppression as someone who is marginalized. Jesus said he would recover sight for the blind. Someone who believes they already see perfectly and have an enlightened perspective won't have a use for that aspect of freedom either.

What about someone who lives in the inner city who has become a Christian? Do the promises of Jesus take on a different meaning? I'm betting yes.

If I pose this question to an African American, Hispanic, or poor white believer, the answers come quickly and with conviction. Freedom in Christ for minorities in our country include the joy found in salvation, but living in the promise and freedom of being "one" in the body of Christ is not their reality.

So, the question is, where does your freedom lie? Where is it that you believe you are free, but in reality, you are not free at all? A follow-up question is, can you see others in your community who are believers but aren't free?

No matter who you are, Jesus has good news for wherever you are poor. You may be poor of self-esteem, poor of wisdom, poor of love, or poor of perspective, which leads to Jesus' good news about recovering your spiritual sight.

Jesus promises to set you free from whatever prison has you locked up. If it is work, Jesus can set you free. If you are in a prison of mental illness, Jesus can set you free. If you are in a prison of selfishness, unforgiveness, or even greed, Jesus can set you free. The oppression for most who don't believe they are oppressed is in adhering to the status quo, which is constantly telling us that change is bad.

Poor and oppressed Christians worship on Sundays just like you and I, but many of them experience Monday through Saturday as the disenfranchised part of the body of Christ. As segregation in the body of Christ continues to mirror segregation in society, the poor and disinherited may be free spiritually, but justice, opportunity, and living in equality with other believers is still elusive.

The contemporary church needs to have its heart broken for those who are believers but are still living in bondage to systemic oppression. A trip down to the "poor" part of town or volunteering one day a year to leave church on Sunday to go help someone in need is not enough. It takes a commitment of time. It takes asking God for direction in this specific area of kinship and reconciliation. It takes being willing to admit that perhaps you have strayed away from the whole gospel that Jesus proclaimed in Luke 4. Sometimes it even takes admitting that you or your church has gotten some of its theology wrong. (I won't hold my breath.)

Pretending as if everything is okay is one way forward, but retracing our steps back to Jesus and rediscovering the simplicity of the gospel may lead the body of Christ forward in a refreshing new way.

Chapter 6

More Than a Brief Moment

**It's time to stop making the case for Christ
and start living the cause of Christ.**

Defending the faith is important. Knowing why you believe is also important. I'm passionate about apologetics and making the case for Jesus, but if making the case doesn't lead to living the life, then I've missed the point.

It is easy for today's believers to get caught up in constantly having to make the case for Christ and against the perceived threats of other religions, science, and governmental interference. Some mistakenly lash out against those who question the divinity of Jesus and others who don't agree with the faith. Meanwhile their local communities become more divided, violent, and broken.

Is there a better way forward? What if our narrative about Jesus being the way could become more visible and less verbal?

Do not lie to each other, since you have taken off your old self with its practices and have put on the new self, which

being renewed in knowledge in the image of its Creator. Here there is no Gentile or Jew, circumcised or uncircumcised, barbarian, Scythian, slave or free, but Christ is all, and is in all. Colossians 3:9–11

The very first words in this passage, "Do not lie," are so compelling for today's believers. When it comes to racial reconciliation, we lie to ourselves every time we turn a blind eye to racism, injustice, and the divisions in the body of Christ. We also lie to each other when we make excuses or justifications for why these things happen instead of standing up and taking responsibility for carrying our brothers' and sisters' burdens. Colossians tells us there are no longer geographical, ethnic, or economic boundaries to abide by. We are all in Christ. Together. Period.

If the letter to the Colossians were written today, it might read: "Here there is no American, or Mexican, Black or White Trash, or Coloreds; no rich or poor, Fox or CNN, Democrat or Republican. But there are only those in Christ, and Christ is in all of us." Yet we allow these markers to define us, divide us, and prevent us from living in and experiencing the shalom of God.

Shalom, or the "wholeness" of peace and balance that is desired by God for His children and creation, is available and coming. It is available in part now, and in eternity it will be experienced in full.

Where Is "Here" and How Do We Get There?

In my walk with Christ since 1999, I have experienced growth, setbacks, and humility all while pursuing an authentic Christian life. Over the last few years I have come to realize this pursuing of Christ is of most importance if maturity and reconciliation with our neighbor is to become a reality.

It seems God through the Holy Spirit deposits a yearning of sorts in the hearts of believers for a destination and fulfillment this side of heaven that can only be realized when willing to surrender each day. Too many Christians stop this pursuit when faced with the uncomfortable tension between classism, status, and race versus the kingdom view of equality, equity, and new creation.

The pursuit of racial reconciliation within the body of Christ calls for pushing through the tension and getting to the place where unity, equality, and spiritual kinship are all that's left.

Colossians reminds us that we have taken or are taking off something old and putting on something new—the old self and its practices. Once this process begins, we are a new creation in a new "here." The old reality with all its labels, status groups, and hierarchy is gone. The "here" is a reference to being in Christ.

The part of God's shalom that is available now is powerful and life altering. Many Christians claim to want peace or to be a peacemaker but perhaps have missed a key ingredient in their search. The key ingredient is biblical reconciliation. Shalom in all our relationships is more than our family, our church, and our local community. Shalom is meant to spread everywhere, with all believers. It is meant to reach into all communities and across all boundaries.

Creation itself cries out for the shalom of God.

We know that the whole creation has been groaning as in the pains of childbirth right up to the present time. Romans 8:22

If Christians would be as bold to groan for the shalom of God as vehemently as they groan against everyone who doesn't agree with their religious or political view, the body of Christ could move mountains. Reconciliation is not just about restored relationships but also about unlocking the power of God to change entire communities.

It's time to ask some important questions.

- Do you believe everything is okay with the body of Christ as is?
- Do you believe there is more that could be done to bring people together and unite as one across all racial, economic, and cultural lines?
- Are you willing to try something different so that future generations of Christians will see the cause of Christ being lived?
- Can you admit you are not experiencing the peace of God in the way you desire?
- Do you believe people on the margins of society who are believers have something to offer?
- Do you believe people on the margins of society who are believers have something you need?

The last question is the most important.

Until believers come to the realization that other believers in their own communities with lesser means, different views, and lesser status have something they need, then nothing will change. What is being sought in the way of growth, identity, and credibility in the contemporary church comes through reconciliation with others in the body of Christ.

God's heart is for reconciling all who are lost; therefore, at some level, God has positioned what *you* need with the believers who are poor, a different color, and do not reflect your worldview.

The mind-set and realities of classism inside the body of Christ must be addressed. A new renewing of the mind is in order. One way to renew our minds is to ask God to break our hearts again for what breaks his. I firmly believe that the acts of racial reconciliation within the contemporary church will set the stage for something much bigger and much better than our present reality.

New Leaders

If God is serious about reconciliation, then I need to be also. He is, and I am.

When I first began to hear "you will be one voice for reconciliation and justice," I was excited. I didn't know what it meant or what the cost would be, but my excitement came because there was such a clarity to the call. I have repeatedly admitted that I am not the only voice. There are many taking up the cause in communities across the country. New leadership is emerging.

I have acquaintances near my hometown who heard the call to plant a multicultural and multiethnic church. They decided to co-pastor this new work by having one white and one African American minister alternating weeks in the pulpit.

I met with a young man who left his position as an associate at a prominent church because of the specific call he heard to go to the inner city and start a church. His former church connected him with an existing church-planting organization to provide resources, but it has been a struggle for him. The young man's question for me was, "Why do the people who are trying to help me continue to hinder me? They keep telling me where to plant based on marketing techniques and the number of people who can be reached. I know where I'm supposed to go, and it's a poor part of town where people are struggling. Why can't they understand this is where I'm supposed to go?"

My answer was simple. I said, "They are used to the status quo, and they don't see it yet, but be patient, because they will."

In my travels around the country to speak in prisons, I have encountered many people who have heard the call for reconciliation within the church. Change is coming for sure, and I believe it will come from the most unlikely of places: it will come from the marginalized and the oppressed.

Change will come from those who are currently incarcerated and hearing the call of God when they are released from prison and go out and heal the body of Christ.

Change will come from the poor who know how to praise God during lean times, without worrying about what it looks like to others, and lead us by example.

Change is coming. Racial reconciliation is the opportunity the body of Christ can no longer afford to overlook.

So Now What?

As part of my new calling, God is giving me new ideas all the time for how reconciliation can begin. Here are a few ideas that I share with others who are hearing the call to racial reconciliation within the body of Christ.

The New Mentorship Model

I strongly urge white pastors, lay leaders, and others in the majority to stop being a mentor to others and find a spiritual mentor of color. I suggest that you invest the next twelve to eighteen months spending time with this person. Your mentor does not have to be older than you, but I would suggest they not be younger. The important aspect of this relationship is that your mentor is one of color and can shed light on things you need to know. (I'm assuming we all have things to learn.)

Do not let this relationship be a two-way mentorship. Sit and listen. Sit at the feet of your brother or sister and lean in and listen. Listen deeply and listen even harder when it becomes uncomfortable. Every time you get the urge to speak, don't.

Ask your mentor to suggest books you should read and then read them. Don't lie about it and say you read them because your mentor will know. Also, resist the temptation to tell others what you are learning for as long as possible.

During those twelve to eighteen months, meditate on Scriptures that talk about the gospel and what it means for all of us. Revisit God's call for reconciliation and how much deeper it goes than simply tolerating each other or being cordial to one another. There is a deeper power hidden within the body of Christ that can only be unleashed when those of us in the majority stop caring about how and trying to direct how do it.

Eventually a new relationship will emerge with your mentor, and it will be one of kinship and burden bearing.

Christian Exchange Program (CXP)

It is no secret that many denominations and other community-based churches have a vision for launching new churches or campuses. I'm all for starting new churches in new locations, but the truth is that predominantly white Christian churches assume it's their right to go anywhere they deem logical or even profitable. Just because an established church has the resources and can get a good deal on an old building or piece of property doesn't necessarily equate to a call to create yet another replica there of what is being done in the suburbs.

When I returned from sabbatical, I had an idea for a new way to launch multiracial churches. It's a model that I believe would bring God honor because it encompasses the kingdom mind-set and forces the body of Christ to work together. I call it the CXP, or Christian Exchange Program. It takes commitment and prayer and a willingness to see it all the way through, but the results would no doubt glorify God in a fresh new way!

Here is the concept. Instead of a suburban church carving out thirty to fifty members to go and start a new campus or church, they would instead become part of an existing inner-city church.

Here is how it works:

- Senior Pastor identifies and builds a relationship with an inner-city pastor who is willing to participate.
- Prayer and discernment take place between the "sending" church and the "receiving church" for at least six months.
- Sending church seeks 5 to 7 percent of its congregation to pray about being sent to become part of the receiving church.

- Those who hear the call to go sign a covenant for a two-year commitment to attend the inner-city church, agree to tithe there, agree to *not* seek any leadership role, agree to volunteer, and agree to journal the experience.

At the end of the two years, if those who went wish to return to their former church, they are welcome to do so. (I wonder if they would.)

Going and Being With

There are several other areas in which the journey to racial reconciliation can begin to take place. Here are a few:

- Go on mission trip to your local courthouse. Sit and observe what happens and what is said. Don't categorize or label anyone, but rather listen intently at the pain beneath the stories. Reflect and pray. Ask God for what's next.
- If you already are volunteering at a local mission or soup kitchen, take one extra step the next time you go. Ask one or more people who come there for aid to tell you their story. No matter how long it takes, don't interrupt and don't chime in. Just listen.
- Call your local sheriff and ask what county jail programs are available for inmates and if you can help. Go and see what God is doing with the poor, the prisoner, and the oppressed. Go and be present with someone who has no hope so they can see hope in you.

- Find a mentor of color or seek guidance and books to read from those who may know about racism and the church. Journal your experiences. Don't be afraid.

The suggestions here in this book are just the tip of the iceberg when it comes to living out the reality of the new "here" described in Colossians 3 through racial reconciliation. The key is going and being with for as long as it takes.

Use these ideas to affirm what God may be saying to you. I do not own the market on ideas for racial reconciliation and new leadership methods. Pray and ask God for direction.

I'll offer a few cautions. First, resist the temptation to turn what you do into another event or outreach from your church. Don't get me wrong, you can go with a group of people from your church, but leave your denominational banner, doctrine, and religious words at home. Go as a true ambassador of the kingdom of God and be vulnerable to experiencing something new in your faith. It comes down to leaving whatever you consider as status behind and meeting the disenfranchised on their turf.

Second, make tangible changes as God leads. For racial reconciliation to gain momentum, more is required than periodic outreach events for those in need or prayer walks in the inner city. The tangible change is for leaders in the white church and their congregations to lay down their assumptions and go and reconcile with the marginalized in their communities.

To lay down assumptions is difficult. It means listening without trying to fix. It requires admitting mistakes and repentance for allowing racial divide to continue for far too long. Finally, and perhaps most difficult for those who embrace the status quo in the body of Christ, racial reconciliation requires a willingness to follow instead of lead.

The responsibility to model racial reconciliation, restorative justice, and kinship is the responsibility of the church.

Amazing things happen when you are in the presence of Jesus, and Jesus is always with the disinherited.

The possibilities are limitless.

The world is watching and waiting.

Reflections and Discussion

I have the privilege of working with some very talented people in ministry, and I have met none more talented than award-winning documentary maker and photographer Todd Scoggins. Scoggins has a giant heart for the kingdom as well as a giant shelf in his studio where his awards are displayed. His studio, I should probably mention, is a converted garage that hardly anyone knows about, which means not many people know about the awards either.

When I travel with Scoggins, we often share stories with each other relating to our experiences in ministry and mission work. One story Scoggins shared with me was about his award-winning documentary *Mission Appalachia: The Story of Red Bird*.

Scoggins knew he was close to the "hollar" where he was supposed to film but couldn't quite find the access road. He recalled, "I went to the end of an old road and found a person sitting on their porch. I politely asked if they could point in which direction was the holler called Red Bird. The person obliged and said, "Head back down the road until you come to Collet's Grocery Store and then head north. The next hollar you come to will be Red Bird."

Scoggins continued, "I went back down the road looking for Collet's Grocery, but I couldn't find it." When he saw another person walking along, he asked, "Can you point me to the access road that leads to Red Bird?" The person said, "Head back up the road until you see Collet's Grocery and you'll see the access road."

Scoggins was beside himself. He could not locate this local landmark called Collet's that everyone else seem to know. Frustration was building, and he needed to find Collet's to go to the next step of his journey.

Finally, off in the distance, something caught his eye. Through the brush and overgrowth, he saw what looked like a vacant lot. As he approached, he saw the partial remains of an old sign lying on the ground. It read: Collet's Grocery.

Neither of the individuals Scoggins had spoken with bothered to tell him that the store had been closed for years. The locals knew where it was, but to an outsider it was all but invisible.

If someone asked you where to find the unified, loving body of Christ today, where would you direct them? What if someone with no status, no resources, and of a different ethnicity asks where to find a place of refuge and hope? If you point them to a church, will it be easy to find? Or has it become like "Collet's Grocery" store, hiding in the weeds and barely visible to those who need transformation and hope?

When the phrase "the church" is spoken, assumptions are made. Some think of a building, and some are thinking of the traditions inside the building. No matter your definition, the dangerous assumption made by most is that those who are seeking hope will find it in what is known as "the church" today. People looking for hope and refuge found in Christ might find hot coffee, slick videos, and people dressed casually, but finding the hope of Christ leading to biblical reconciliation could be elusive.

Discussion Prompts

Use these prompts to begin conversations for awareness, healing, and change. Add other questions as God leads.

1. Do you think the identity of "the church" as a unified, set apart, world-changing movement has become unrecognizable to the disenfranchised? Why?
2. How can the overall church in America move towards a more equal, equitable, and authentic reflection of the gospel?
3. Picturing the community in which you live, name the things that encourage you and the things that discourage you.
4. Picturing a community near you that is poorer, has less opportunity, and a higher crime rate; name things that you believe discourage the people living in that community who profess to be Christian?
5. Write out a working definition of what you believe *racial reconciliation* is and then list three things you can do that will help the body of Christ move in the direction of your definition.

Notes

1. Page 11: Pew Research Center
   Article July 2015, "Diversity/Mainline Church."

2. Page 13: "It cannot be overstated that too often . . ."
   Howard Thurman, *Jesus and the Disinherited* (Boston: Beacon Press, 1976), 20.

3. Page 27: "the opportunity to mourn what our communities look like…"
   Soong-Chan Rah, *The Prophetic Lament: A Call for Justice in Troubled Times* (Downers Grove: Intervarsity Press, 2015), 47.

4. Page 32: "What we understand about the Old Testament…"
   Walter Brueggemann, *The Prophetic Imagination* (Minneapolis: Fortress Press, 2001), 1.

5. Page 52: "African American women have never thought of themselves…"
   Elizabeth Conde-Frazier, S. Steve Kang, and Gary A. Parrett, *A Many Colored Kingdom: Multicultural Dynamics for Spiritual Formation.* (Grand Rapids: Baker Academic, 2001), 91.

6. Page 52: "Mexican Americans have internalized shame and guilt…"
   Elizabeth Conde-Frazier, S. Steve Kang, and Gary A. Parrett, *A Many Colored Kingdom: Multicultural Dynamics for Spiritual Formation.* (Grand Rapids: Baker Academic, 2001), 92.

Acknowledgements

I am often amazed at the number of people who have made a profound impact on my life. Sometimes, I think about how blessed I am by the people God chose to bring into my life for the long haul, seasons of growth, and even the short-term spiritual ninjas who are here and gone in the blink of an eye. I have had no lack of very smart, compassionate, and spirit filled people who have shaped me over the years. I am forever grateful.

When deciding to write this book, I understood that calling on past experiences and lessons learned from people in my life would be important. I never imagined, however, once I began writing, the difficult emotional journey I was embarking upon and therefore my need for guidance and spiritual support.

I want to thank those who played a key role in the development of the book and bringing the best out of me when I was all but ready to lay it down.

First, I thank Claudia May, PhD, who challenged me in 2016 at the Institute for Reconciliation at Duke Divinity School, to go back to Indiana and seek out a mentor of color. I made good on that promise, and I will be forever grateful to Claudia for her fearless pursuit of becoming more like Jesus every day.

Subsequently, the next person I acknowledge and thank is Pastor Louis Jackson Jr. Pastor Louis is the mentor of color that God led me to in 2016 who affirmed my call and passion for racial reconciliation. Thank you, Louis, for your trust in me, the honesty of conversation, and your courage to keep going in your quest for unity in the body of Christ. I am so thankful to pastor Louis, his wife Bea, and the entire United In Christ Church family.

A big thank you to Shawn O'Connor, who provided feedback as well as planted new seeds of thought that took root and began to sprout in my spirit at just the right times. Shawn O'Connor is a chaplain at Pendleton Juvenile Correctional facility in Indiana. Shawn and his family live out the gospel every day, and their witness has often served to hold me to a higher standard of believer and human being.

I thank Dan'l Markham, preacher, author, radio and TV personality, and consultant in beautiful Mt. Vernon, Washington. I admire Dan'l and respect his work in fighting social injustices with nothing more than the gospel as a weapon. Thank you, Dan'l, for not allowing me to settle. I appreciate your honesty and encouragement throughout the process and will always be grateful for our friendship.

Thank you to Dr. Agee, Professor of Church History at Anderson University. You were a divine appointment for me on a day when I wasn't sure anyone cared about racial reconciliation in the body of Christ. Thank you for being where you were and saying what you said. You'll never understand what it meant to me.

Thank you to Sam Linette; an ordained pastor at Common Ground Christian Church in Northeast Indianapolis. I am grateful for your feedback, your friendship, and the way you continue taking the steps of faith the Lord has laid out for you.

I also thank Pastor Rakshan Cain (Rock), who I recently had the privilege of meeting. Rock is one of many campus pastors at

Christ Fellowship Church in Port St. Lucie, Florida. I instantly made a kinship connection with Rock, and I am forever grateful for your willingness to read my work and offer your honest and loving critique.

Finally, I thank my family. To my children, I thank you for listening to me talk about this book for a long time. I thank you for allowing me to retreat to my room at night and begin writing, only to take a 30-minute break and yell out answers to Jeopardy, most of which were wrong. Thank you to my wife, Shelley. You have helped me more than you know by listening, encouraging, and allowing me to process "out loud" (even though it often makes no sense). I love you.

Thank you, Mom, for always supporting me and loving me. You really are the best mom in the world and I always want to be more like you when it comes to kindness, compassion, and serving. Oh, and...I love you more.

We lost my Dad in February 2018, but I want to acknowledge his part in who I am as a pastor, writer, and person. I began writing this book and the series that will follow in late 2017 while my Father was still alive. I am thankful for my dad's character and what he instilled in me as man. Never did he pretend to be perfect, but he was always truthful and straight to the point. My father grew up in a town that had its fair share of racism, classism, and religious hypocrisy. But to my knowledge, my father treated everyone with respect to the best of his ability.

At my father's visitation, the line at the funeral home was four hours long. As the evening began to come to an end, I noticed the last person in line was an elderly black man. He had waited patiently to have a few moments to pay his respects. As he stepped forward as the last person in line, I shook his hand and said, "Thank you so much for waiting so long. It means so much to us and I'm sure it would have meant a lot to my dad." The elderly black man replied, "If a man can't wait a few hours to pay respect to another man, a man like your father, then what's life come to?"

My father never stood on a soapbox and preached about racial reconciliation. He didn't have to. He simply treated people the way he wanted to be treated. Thank you, Dad. You are loved and missed.

Resources

- www.jayharveyministries.me

- www.reconciliationacademy.com

- Book series: *Reconciling All Things:
  A Christian Vision for Justice, Peace, and Healing*
  Emmanuel Katongole & Chris Rice; (IVP Books)

- The Center for Reconciliation, Duke Divinity School
  www.dukereconciliation.com

Book 2: What's Coming Next

When I began writing this book, my relationship with Pastor Louis Jackson Jr. was still somewhat new. The awareness of what God was doing in our relationship, however, was obvious to both of us. I was growing rapidly in my understanding of what reconciliation is all about, and Louis became increasingly more comfortable in sharing his experiences with me along with his passion for unity in the body of Christ.

Since March 2017, I have launched a new inner-city church, continued meeting with Louis, and expanded my prison ministry by serving as an adjunct speaker for the Life Without Limbs Global Prison Ministry based in Ventura, California.

Bringing racial reconciliation to the forefront in the body of Christ, I understand, will be an ongoing process and a journey filled with new discoveries as well as burdens. There is so much to share and so much work to be done. I found myself adding and revising to this book several times in the past several months after I thought I was mostly finished because of all that I was learning and experiencing. I eventually decided not to try and cram everything into one book. It would be impossible.

So I invite you to stay connected with me and watch for two more books in this series. The next two books will contain stories from those I have been interviewing in prisons, the addicted, and people who have been marginalized within the body of Christ.

Made in the USA
Monee, IL
29 June 2024